My First
American Friend

Story by Sarunna Jin
Illustrations by Shirley V. Beckes

RSVP

RAINTREE
STECK-VAUGHN
PUBLISHERS
The Steck-Vaughn Company

Austin, Texas

献给我亲爱的外祖父,外祖母。

To my dearest grandfather and grandmother
with all my love and thanks. —S.J.

To my first friend. —S.B.

Trade Edition published 1992 © Steck-Vaughn Company
Copyright © 1992 Steck-Vaughn Company

Copyright © 1991 Raintree Publishers Limited Partnership

4 5 6 7 8 9   94 93

Library of Congress Number: 90-41471

Library of Congress Cataloging-in-Publication Data

Jin, Sarunna.
   My first American friend / story by Sarunna Jin; illustrations by Shirley V.
Beckes.

   Summary: A young Chinese girl beginning a new life in America
finds the difficult adjustment more endurable when she makes her first
American friend.
   (1. Chinese Americans—Fiction.   2. Friendship—Fiction.)   I. Beckes,
Shirley V., ill.   II. Title.
PZ7.J5756My   1990   (E)—dc20   90-41471
ISBN 0-8172-2785-7 hardcover library binding   CIP
ISBN 0-8114-4310-8 softcover binding   AC

I was born in China. When I was two months old, I went to live with my grandparents in a place called Inner Mongolia in China. This made it possible for my parents to go to school in a different part of China. They wanted to do this so that we could all have a better life someday.

Later, my parents went to America to study at a school called Boston College. It is in the state of Massachusetts. I stayed with my grandparents in China. I was happy there with them and my friends.

When I was six years old, my parents asked me if I would like to join them in America. I said, "Okay!"

On the morning of my journey to America, I had to get up at five o'clock. My grandma and I traveled by train to Beijing, the capital of China. There we met my aunt, who took us to the airport. Even though I was so young, I was flying to America all by myself!

The trip was a real adventure. I flew from China to Japan, and from Japan to San Francisco in America. From there I flew to New York, where my mom and dad were waiting. We had a happy reunion with hugs and kisses.

Soon after I got to America, I started first grade. I didn't know any English. That made it difficult for me to do everything. I tried to talk with the other children, but we could not understand each other.

No one played with me. Oh, how sad and lonely I was for my friends that I had left behind. I felt especially sad when my mom read a letter from my grandmother. It said that one of my friends in China had knocked on my grandmother's door and asked, "Is Sarunna back yet?" That made me sadder. Then something happened to make me feel better.

I was sitting at my desk during playtime when a girl named Ali came over to play with me. Ali had blue eyes, a pretty smile, and beautiful blonde hair. I had never seen such pretty hair before. Even though I could only speak a little bit of English, Ali and I had lots of fun together. She let me touch her pretty hair.

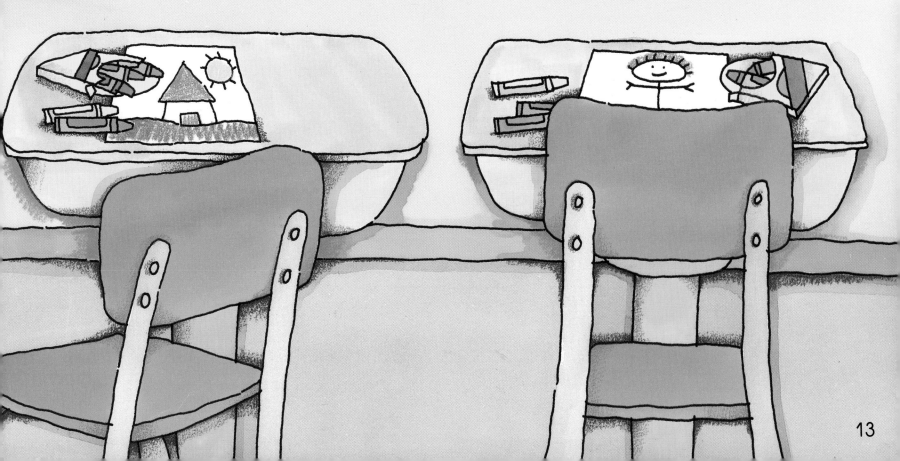

From that day on, we always played together at school. Sometimes we played on the swings. Sometimes we played on the slide.

In the classroom, we built blocks and painted together. Ali and I became best friends and were very happy!

16

At the end of the year, Ali told me that she was moving to another school. I was sad again because my very best friend was leaving. On the last day of school, we hugged and said good-bye.

18

In second grade, my English improved a lot. I still had some problems with the language, but I made many new friends.

This year, I am in the third grade, and my English is perfect! I have many friends now, and I'm very happy. But I'll always remember Ali, my first American friend.

74976

From the time she was two months old, Sarunna Jin was raised by her grandparents in China so that her parents could devote themselves to their educations. **My First American Friend** is the true story of how Sarunna's life changed greatly at age six, when she was reunited with her parents in America.

When Sarunna arrived in America, she longed for her family and friends in her homeland, particularly her grandparents. Sarunna had difficulties adjusting to a new and different world until she met her very first and unforgettable American friend, Ali.

Sarunna spoke no English upon her arrival in America. When she wrote **My First American Friend** in third grade, she had been speaking English only 2½ years. She became accomplished in English through the English As A Second Language program and her classroom studies at John Ward School in Newton, Massachusetts. The school highly encourages reading, writing, and the study of literature.

Reading is Sarunna's favorite subject. She also enjoys swimming, ice skating, playing the piano and the recorder, gymnastics, and riding her bicycle. She wants to be a medical doctor when she grows up.

Sarunna's parents are Jingmin and Erdan Jin.

Soon after Sarunna and Ali became friends, Ali had to move away to another city. After a two-year separation, Sarunna and Ali were reunited at the Young Publish-A-Book award ceremony.

The ten honorable-mention winners in the **1990 Raintree Young Publish-A-Book Contest** were: Kara Brun of Glendale, Arizona; Debra Buchanan of Garden Grove, California; Oscar Chavez of Wilmington, California; Nikki Chun of Honolulu, Hawaii; Cindy Knoebel of Marquette, Michigan; David Martinez of Citrus Heights, California; Sarah Maxell of Portland, Maine; Megan McCoy of Hot Springs, Arkansas; Michelle Parnau of Greenfield, Wisconsin; and Kenosha Seaberry of Milwaukee, Wisconsin.

Artist Shirley V. Beckes has been illustrating children's books for seventeen years. She graduated from Columbus College of Art and Design. Shirley, her husband, David, and their daughter, Jennifer, live in the Milwaukee area, where she and David have their studio, Beckes Design/Illustration.